D0853145

WE CAN READ!™

Lava

by Jacqueline Sweeney

photography by G. K. & Vikki Hart
photo illustration by Blind Mice Studio

BENCHMARK BOOKS

MARSHALL CAVENDISH
NEW YORK

For Adam Markovics, who's been bubbling
in leftover fires—can't put 'em out—yet
still comes through!

With thanks to Daria Murphy, principal of Scotchtown
Elementary School, Goshen, New York,
and former reading specialist, for reading this
manuscript with care and for writing the
"We Can Read and Learn" activity guide.

Benchmark Books
Marshall Cavendish
99 White Plains Road
Tarrytown, New York 10591
www.marshallcavendish.com

Text copyright © 2003 by Jacqueline Sweeney
Photo illustrations © 2003 by G.K. & Vikki Hart
and Mark and Kendra Empey

Library of Congress Cataloging-in-Publication Data
Sweeney, Jacqueline.
Lava / by Jacqueline Sweeney ; photography by G.K. and Vikki Hart ;
photo illustration by Blind Mice Studio.
p. cm. -- (We can read!)
Summary: Kono Gecko takes his animal friends for a walk to see a volcano.
ISBN 0-7614-1511-4
[1. Volcanoes—Fiction. 2. Geckos—Fiction. 3. Hawaii—Fiction.]
I. Hart, G. K., ill. II. Hart, Vikki, ill. III. Title.
PZ7.S974255 Lav 2002   [E]—dc21   2002074752

Printed in Italy

1 3 5 6 4 2

Characters

Kono

Hildy

Molly

Ladybug

Gus

Kono Gecko woke up early.

Chick-Chak!

Chick-Chak!

"Wake up, lazybones!" he chirped.

Hildy yawned.

Molly rubbed her eyes.

"Today we holo-holo," said Kono.

Ladybug fluttered, "What's that?"

"It means to take a walk," said Kono.

"And this walk is a surprise."

He leaped out the door.

The friends walked all morning.
They passed tall palm trees and
fields of wild grass.

They hiked on long beaches
of white and black sand.

And always, the sea was beside them.

"The sea is like music," said Hildy.

"The sea *is* music," said Kono.

"It's also a friend.

But it's time to head up."

Up they climbed
over chunky black rocks.
"This hurts my knees," groaned Gus.
"Don't stop!" said Kono.
"We're almost there."

"Almost where?" asked Molly.

But Kono didn't answer.

"He's hiding again," quacked Hildy.

"He'll be back."

The friends kept walking.

"I'm sweating," said Molly.

"I'm thirsty," groaned Gus.

"It's too hot!"

"Look at the rocks!" cried Ladybug.

"They're steaming!"

"Where ARE we?" shouted Molly.

"And where's Kono?"

"I'm worried," said Hildy.

"He's been gone too long."

RUMBLE

RUMBLE

The friends stopped and listened.

RUMBLE

RUMBLE

"There it is again," said Molly.

"We have to find Kono!"

quacked Hildy.

"He might be hurt."

Hildy and Ladybug flew off.

Molly bit her nails.
Gus hid in his shell.
They waited and waited.
It got very dark.

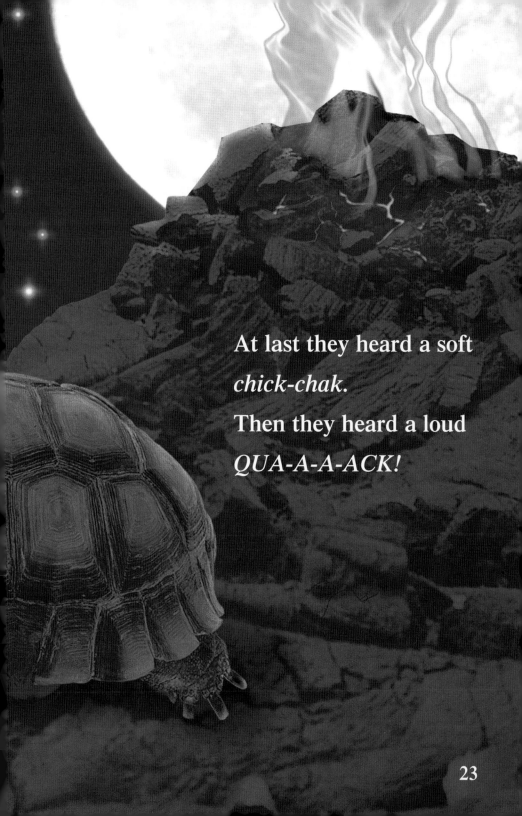

At last they heard a soft
chick-chak.
Then they heard a loud
QUA-A-A-ACK!

23

Gus and Molly shouted with joy.
Hildy plopped down beside them.
Kono and Ladybug
lay on her back.

"I'm sorry I scared you,"
said Kono.
"I was hiding. But I got lost."

25

"Are you ready for the surprise?" asked Kono.

"We're on a volcano.

Soon lava will shoot into the sky!"

"Is it safe?" asked Gus.

"Oh yes," said Kono.

"We're still far away."

The friends watched the sky.
RUMBLE
RUMBLE
BOOM!
Lava flowed down the mountain
and into the sea.

Kono sighed. "This is how islands are made—in Hawaii."

WE CAN READ AND LEARN

The following activities, which complement *Lava*, are designed to help children build skills in vocabulary, phonics, critical thinking, and creative writing.

HOT LAVA CHALLENGE WORDS

Cut flowing rivers of lava from red construction paper and write the words below (all of which appear in *Lava*) on these lava flows. Line a glass vase with blue construction paper. The vase will be the sea into which the lava flows will run. Discuss the meaning of a word written on a lava flow, then ball up the lava flow and place it into the sea. Gradually, the vase will fill up and the balled-up flows will begin to stick out. Explain that a new island has come out of the sea, formed by the cooling, piling, and cementing of lava flows. This may be a good starting point for an in-depth discussion of the different types of volcanoes and how they work.

lazybones	surprise	palm	fields
wild	hiked	beaches	sea
always	chunky	black	rocks
hurts	knees	sweating	thirsty
steaming	worried	rumble	volcano
lava	shoot	flowed	mountain
islands			

SANDY SURPRISES

In this story, the friends walked on sandy beaches. Children can create sand plaster molds to hang up or use as decorative paperweights. Foam meat trays (small ones work best), sand, plaster, large paper clips, shells, beads, sea glass, feathers, and other beach mementos are all that is needed. Use a foam tray as a base. Cover it completely with sand. Add shells, beads, and other items, pressing them into the sand gently but firmly. Carefully pour pre-mixed plaster over the set pieces. Insert a large paper clip into the top at an angle (this will become a hook for hanging). Allow the plaster to harden thoroughly. Peel off the foam tray and gently brush aside the loose sand. A sandy surprise is in your hands.

ISLANDS IN THE SEA AND SUN

Hawaii is made up of many islands. Children can use clay to create their own chain of islands, naming each one after a friend or family member. Create a special history explaining how each island was formed. Record the information on paper chains, glue them together, and surround the new islands with sea, sun, and a chain of information.

FUN WITH READING STRATEGIES

An important strategy for beginning readers is to learn to find little words they recognize within larger, unfamiliar, words. Cut big and little flows of lava from red paper. Write the little words and the larger, related words on the lava flows. Have children match the little flow to the larger flow that it is a part of.

each/beach   rub/rubbed   out/shouted   day/today
or/morning   and/sand   way/always   an/answer

VULCANOLOGISTS REPORTING FOR DUTY

Children can learn more about volcanoes by creating a book of volcano facts. Cut sheets of white paper into a volcano shape. On each sheet, record important facts about the workings of volcanoes and add illustrations. Add pages about famous volcanoes such as Kilauea, Vesuvius, and Mount St. Helens. Design a cover for the book and bind with staples, yarn or binder rings.

Children also can learn about volcanoes by creating their own "volcanic" eruptions. Make a volcano out of clay or plaster. Insert a metal or plastic cylinder through its center. Add baking soda to the center. Then add white vinegar. Add red food coloring for a more realistic effect. Watch the lava flow!

About the author

Jacqueline Sweeney is a poet and children's author. She has worked with children and teachers for over twenty-five years implementing writing workshops in schools throughout the United States. She specializes in motivating reluctant writers and shares her creative teaching methods in numerous professional books for teachers. Her most recent work includes the Benchmark Books series *Kids Express*, a series of anthologies of poetry and art by children, which she conceived of and edited. She lives in Catskill, New York.

About the photo illustrations

The photo illustrations are the collaborative effort of photographers G. K. and Vikki Hart and Mark and Kendra Empey of Blind Mice Studio. Following Mark Empey's sketched storyboard, G. K. and Vikki Hart photograph each animal and element individually. The images are then scanned and manipulated, pixel by pixel, by Mark and Kendra Empey at Blind Mice Studio. Each charming illustration may contain from 15 to 30 individual photographs.

All the animals that appear in this book were handled with love. They have been returned to or adopted by loving homes.

32